# Inch by Inch

# Inch by Inch

### Leo Lionni

*Dragonfly Books* · *New York*

One day a hungry robin saw an inchworm, green as an emerald, sitting on a twig. He was about to gobble him up.

"Don't eat me. I am an inchworm. I am useful.
I measure things."
"Is that so!" said the robin. "Then measure my tail!"

"That's easy," said the inchworm.
"One, two, three, four, five inches."

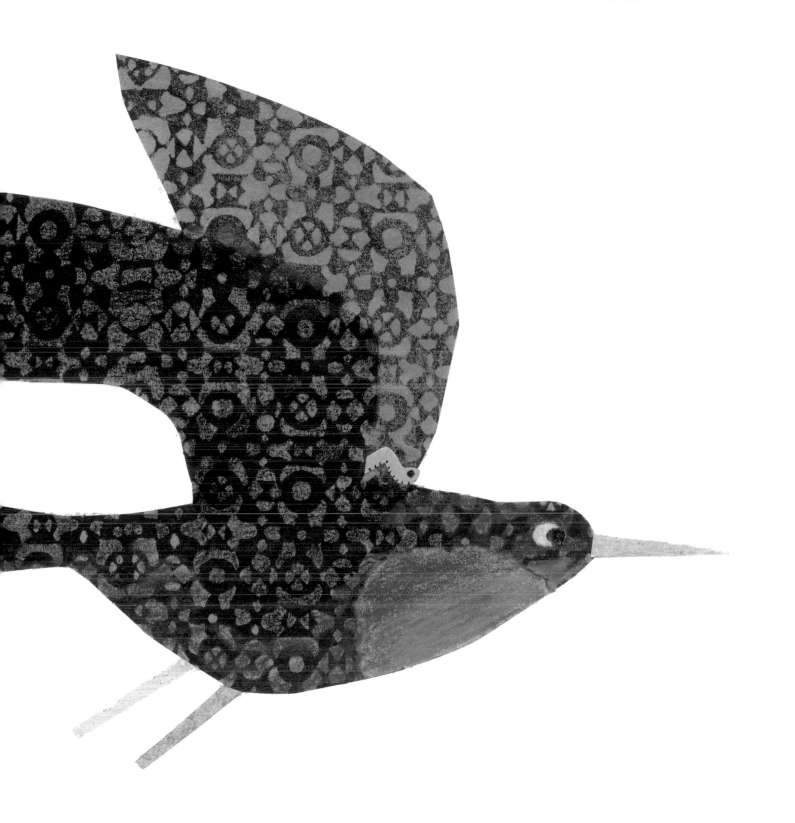

"Just think," said the robin, "my tail is five inches long!"
And with the inchworm, he flew to where other birds needed to be measured.

The inchworm measured the neck of the flamingo.

He measured the toucan's beak . . .

the legs of the heron . . .

the tail of the pheasant . . .

and the whole hummingbird.

One morning, the nightingale met the inchworm.

"Measure my song," said the nightingale.

"But how can I do that?" said the inchworm. "I measure things, not songs."

"Measure my song or I'll eat you for breakfast," said the nightingale.

Then the inchworm had an idea.

"I'll try," he said, "go ahead and sing."

The nightingale sang and the inchworm measured away.

He measured and measured . . .

Inch by Inch . . .

until he inched out of sight.

All rights reserved. Published in the United States by Dragonfly Books, an imprint of Random House Children's Books, a division of Penguin Random House LLC, New York. Originally published in hardcover in the United States by Alfred A. Knopf, an imprint of Random House Children's Books, New York, in 1960.

Dragonfly Books with the colophon is a registered trademark of Penguin Random House LLC.

Visit us on the Web! rhcbooks.com

Educators and librarians, for a variety of teaching tools, visit us at RHTeachersLibrarians.com

The Library of Congress has cataloged the hardcover edition of this work as follows:
Lionni, Leo, 1910–1999.
Inch by inch / by Leo Lionni.
p.   cm.
Summary: To keep from being eaten, an inchworm measures a robin's tail, a flamingo's neck, a toucan's beak, a heron's legs, and a nightingale's song.
ISBN 978-0-375-85764-5 (trade) — ISBN 978-0-375-95764-2 (lib. bdg.)
[1. Caterpillars—Fiction. 2. Birds—Fiction.] I. Title.
PZ7.L6634Ip 2010
[E]—dc22
2009001767

ISBN 978-1-5247-6614-6 (pbk.)

MANUFACTURED IN CHINA

10 9 8 7 6 5

First Dragonfly Books Edition